Bella Vista Books, LLC.

the Sand Dollar

MICHAEL WOODWORTH
illustrated by CRAIG PENNINGTON

Production Date: September, 2011
Production Location: Printed by Everbest Printing
(Guangzhou, China), Co. Ltd.
Job/Batch #: 99807

Library of Congress Control Number: 2011915836
ISBN   978-0-9836726-0-9

Acknowledgment

To Jim and Susan who called me to the Sea of Cortez
and to Gina who taught me to hear its voice.
And a very special thanks to Ray.

A man walked among colorful shells scattered on the shore of the Sea of Cortez.

As he walked, the sea rolled in gentle waves and cool water slid against his bare feet.

From time to time the man stopped, reached down and picked up a shell to look at it more closely.

Some of the shells he put into his pocket. Most of them he left behind on the wet sand.

Just as the man was about to end his journey,
he spotted a large shell unlike any he had collected.

He moved quickly to the shell, reached down
and stretched out his hand to claim it.

SUDDENLY, a big wave came from the Sea.
It was as HIGH as the man's waist
and washed past him onto the beach.

On its return, the wave lifted the
shell and carried it back to the Sea.
The shell disappeared as the
man watched.

Saddened by his bad luck, the man turned his eyes to the place where the shell had been. There, to his surprise, he saw a SAND DOLLAR.

When the man bent over the sand dollar,

THE SEA ROSE HIGH IN THE AIR.

Waves rolled up and down the shore all around the man but none entered the spot where he stood.

And, even though waves tumbled onto the sand all around him, there was no SOUND.

Then the Sea broke the silence.

"THIS SAND DOLLAR IS MY GIFT TO YOU. PICK IT UP."

The man picked up the sand dollar.

"NOW BREAK THE SAND DOLLAR INTO PIECES."

"But if I break the sand dollar your gift will be ruined," the man said.

"IF YOU DO NOT BREAK THE SAND DOLLAR MY GIFT
WILL BE LOST," replied the Sea.

The man broke the sand dollar in pieces.
FIVE DOVES fell into his hand.

"These doves are beautiful!" the man exclaimed.

"Did you make them for me?"

"NOT YOU ALONE," said the Sea,
"THE SAND DOLLAR HOLDS
MY STORY FOR ALL."

"Tell me," said the man,

"Why are there five doves inside the sand dollar?"

"THOSE ARE DOVES OF PEACE," the Sea replied.
"ONE TO MARK EACH OF MY FIVE GREAT WARS."

"What wars has the Sea had?" asked the man.

"MY FIRST WAR WAS WITH THE SUN," said the Sea.

"THE SUN AND I RAGED AGAINST ONE ANOTHER
FOR THOUSANDS OF YEARS.
THEN WE REACHED A BALANCE THAT
YOU FEEL AS GENTLE WARMTH.

THE FIRST DOVE OF THE SAND DOLLAR MARKS
MY PEACE WITH THE SUN."

"And what was your second war?" asked the man.
" MY SECOND WAR WAS WITH THE WIND.

THE WIND AND I FOUGHT ONE ANOTHER
UNTIL WE COULD FIGHT NO MORE.

THEN WE REACHED A BALANCE THAT
YOU KNOW AS THE OCEAN CURRENTS.

The second dove of the sand dollar marks my peace with the wind."

"And what was your third war?" asked the man.

"MY THIRD WAR WAS WITH THE MOUNTAINS. THE MOUNTAINS AND I BATTLED ONE ANOTHER FROM THE MOMENT THE FIRST ROSE FROM MY DEPTHS. THEN WE REACHED A BALANCE THAT YOU KNOW AS THE COAST.

"The third dove of the sand dollar marks my peace with the mountains."

"And what was your fourth war?" asked the man.

"MY FOURTH WAR WAS WITH THE MOON.
THE MOON AND I PULLED AGAINST ONE ANOTHER
THROUGH COUNTLESS DAYS AND ENDLESS NIGHTS.
THEN WE REACHED A BALANCE THAT YOU
KNOW AS THE TIDES.

THE FOURTH DOVE OF
THE SAND DOLLAR
MARKS MY PEACE
WITH THE MOON."

"And what was your fifth war?"

asked the man.

"MY FIFTH WAR IS WITH MAN,"

replied the Sea.

"But I am not at war with the Sea,"

said the man.

"YES," said the Sea.

"EACH DAY MAN AND I FIGHT ONE ANOTHER
OVER HOW MUCH I HAVE TO GIVE AND HOW
MUCH MAN SEEKS TO TAKE.

THIS WAR HAS NOT ENDED."

"But if this war is not over why are there already five doves in the sand dollar?" asked the man.

"THE NEED FOR FIVE DOVES IS CERTAIN," the Sea answered.

"FOR THE FIFTH DOVE WILL EITHER MARK MY PEACE WITH MAN OR . . .

IT WILL MARK THE PEACE THAT COMES IF MAN'S OWN CARELESSNESS FOREVER REMOVES HIM FROM MY SHORES."